I0669761

Louisa Blake

Supper Flies and Other Pieces

A Christmas Booklet of Original Verse

Louisa Blake

Supper Flies and Other Pieces
A Christmas Booklet of Original Verse

ISBN/EAN: 9783337023164

Printed in Europe, USA, Canada, Australia, Japan

Cover: Foto ©Andreas Hilbeck / pixelio.de

More available books at **www.hansebooks.com**

SUPPER FLIES

AND OTHER PIECES.

A Christmas Booklet of Original Verse

BY

LOUISA BLAKE,

AUTHORESS OF "IN THE ROUGH."

The gathered harvest of a year!
Is't worth the reaping? much I fear,
If any like or love my lay,
To know would be my crowning day.

Christchurch, N.Z.   L. B.

PRICE   ..   ..   ..   ONE SHILLING.

Wellington, N.Z. :

EDWARDS, RUSSELL & Co., Ld., 11 BRANDON STREET.

1895

INDEX.

Supper Flies.

An old man gathered up his scraps,
 For last smoke of the day;
Shook out his pockets, brushed the flaps,
 Lest even dust might stray.

He hobbled out, and set his chair,
 Then watched the evening close,
And fought the spectres, Want and Care,
 That ever nearer rose.

The loveliness of evening smote
 So gently on his heart;
The past rose up, he 'gan to dote
 Of failings on his part.

He raised his poor old eyes a bit,
 And saw a spider weave
His wond'rous web, and deftly hit;
 The old man fell to grieve.

" When I was young, how quick I was
 Of eye, and hand, and brain;
Nor weakness kept me back, because
 I'd strength to bear a strain."

The spider does his work, then rests
 With all his many eyes
Alert, he, patient, waiting guests
 In shape of supper flies,

Which Providence has promised him
    If he but spin aright.
But what is this ?   A spider's whim
    Will end him in a plight.

The air is full of thistle-down
    That, dancing, comes so light,
Quite heedless of the spider's frown,
    Who darts, with all his might,

And seizes it, then fiercely winds
    So safely in his store.
Oh ! silly spider ! on these lines
    Thy supper will be poor.

The old man mused, " How like to me,
    Who, full of daring high,
Industrious wound, so careless, free,
    E'en thistle-down for fly.

" When tide was low I'd hurry fast,
    Not patient, wait for flow ;
And when (as Shakespeare tells) at last
    It rose for me, then lo !

" I was not there, so missed the flood,
    And cared not much I did ;
For over useless things, no good,
    My fellows I'd outbid.

" And now I'm like the spider here,
    With web all tangled up ;
My life's end supperless and drear,
    A flaw'd and breaking cup.

" I wish my story chance might save
    Some merry little lad,
Prevent his chasing thistle, drave
    On winds that blow so mad."

He murmur'd on, and dropt his pipe,
    Empty, from out his hand;
A faulty fruit, sun could not ripe,
    One gently loosed the band.

His grandchild came to kiss good-night,
    Wonder'd he looked so pale ;
Knew not that, in the fading light,
    Kind death had flung his flail.

The Primrose.

A RECOLLECTION.

Truly thou art not "nothing more" to me
When, lingeringly, I gaze on thy star face,
Think how the poets have embalmed thee,
Thy loveliness, the theme they love to grace.

Still it remains for me (unknown) to tell
Of scene which thou from memory dost evoke ;
A picture of thee in thy native dell,
When perfect Spring had perfectly awoke.

Thy crinkled leaves a spreading carpet made,
Rich 'broidered o'er with primrose bud and flower ;
The light-leaved branches threw a flickering shade,
The sun shone through, and fell the soft warm shower.

(Thy sweet evasive scent the air enlaves,
Just barely caught, then faintly dying, spent,
As over sand so breaks the tiny waves,
No sooner touching mark, than they relent).

When moonlight falls on such a scene as here,
One could imagine fairy-land of old ;
But in these factful days our minds are clear,
We own no spell, nor tale so fancy bold.

But primroses, from making no advance,
And still believing that the fairies are,
They come and revel in the joyous dance,
'Til morn's pale light gathers the farthest star.

The happy primrose blooms on distant strand,
So careful planted in the garden fair ;
But, yet, a stranger in a far-off land,
Sadly, at times, recalls the wild-wood's lair.

The Soul's Awakening.

IN HONOUR OF C. P.'S COPY OF J. SANT'S PICTURE.

Divinely beautiful the thought, a Soul awaking,
E'en though to bitter grief aroused by Sorrow's hand ;
Or, by Adversity, who comes with her rough shaking,
So from its eyes but fall, being loosed, the blinding band.

Far other wakening, dear Clare, than mournful one, be thine ;
May lovely Thought, bright Joy and shimmering Hope attend ;
The glorious light of Love, full breaking on thee, shine,
And Faith (as giving thee sight of things unseen) defend.

Then the true morn shall come, thy wakening Soul awakes,
In that far land, full opened eyes shall clearer see ;
All darkening shadows fall, but those that brightness makes,
As thou art from the bandage of earth's clay set free.

A Study from Life.

I've seen the quarried marble standing out
    Most pure and white,
So exquisitely fine, and traced throughout
    With pencillings light ;
As earthly touches make us see the more
Their virtues, who possess a goodly store.

Of sculptors many, passing to and fro,
    Some names I knew,
As Joy or Sorrow, even bitter Woe,
    They, curious grew,
Asked, " Who shall carve this out, so fine a piece ?
The fame of him who does it should increase."

Sorrow, sorrowing said, " 'Twill be my work,
    I know this vein ;
From out the depths of it, where'er they lurk,
    Reveal the grain,
As with my sharpest tools, I chisel long,
The man awakes, distinct amidst the throng."

But first of all the master, bright Joy, bade
    An outline make ;
And after that, he lovely touches laid,
    And forth there break
A form quite beautiful, and many saw
A work most gracious, guiltless of a flaw.

But some, with instinct rare, craved for the best
    From such a mine ;
Saw no completeness there ; unlike the rest
    Said, " 'Tis not fine ;"
So thought the master of the world's workroom,
And bidding Sorrow rise, led 'midst the gloom.

So Sorrow took in hand this marble fine,
    Made no mistake,
But dealt great strokes, so deepening the line,
    As fell each flake
There rose, 'neath rivings sharp, a thing divine,
Fit for a niche in God's most sacred shrine.

And year by year more lovely grew that form ;
    The polished stone
Was perfected, had borne the stress and storm ;
    Its sculptor prone !
And then, at last, comes Victory on wings,
To place a Crown, sent by the King of Kings.

Lark in Cage—New Brighton Pier.

I pity thee, poor pretty bird,
And this thy quivering heart knows well ;
Man took thy life of life, unstirred
When rang thy freedom's funeral knell.

To thee sweet liberty is life,
The power to mount ecstatic joy ;
The bars to one an endless strife
Whose wings were made for Heaven's deploy.

I see thee plume thy lightsome wing,
As though thou longed to upward rise ;
The floor impede thy rushing spring,
The roof an ever sad surprise.

Close to the rolling sea thy cage,
Emblem of freedom thou dost hear,
Unfettered, as it bursts in rage,
Or rippling as thy song, so clear.

I think of all the captives bound,
Of all the bitter, bitter cries ;
And wish we knew that every sound
Went up to God beyond the skies.

These are the moods that tempt to doubt,
These piercing thoughts of many a lot ;
It seems that wrong may cry—nay, shout,
And all the time that He forgot.

Listen, wild bird ! be still my heart !
Above the roaring of the sea,
Dwells One who takes the sufferer's part,
And will set every captive free.

Autumn Evening—Hagley Park.

Come ! 'tis the close of Autumn day,
    And see it die ;
The golden glory cannot stay
    Of such a sky.
The Southern Alps against it stand,
    Blacker than night ;
Their silhouetted outlines grand,
    Enhance the light.
Above, the crescent moon shines fair,
    Like all things young ;
The Koh-i-noor of night is there,
    On blue, forth-sprung.
It takes from all the stars their light,
    They palely gleam ;
The West will gather moon and star from sight,
    As 'twere a dream.

Story of a Cloak.

Across a wintry track, where bitter winds
    Blew 'gainst a man, trod one ;
His well-lined cloak he ever closer binds,
    Loved for long service done ;

And as he drew it round him, facing blast,
    His courage rose, his feet
Were planted firm to conquer this rough cast,
    Rain and the piercing sleet.

Soon from roadside another joined the track,
    Poorer from want of cloak,
And poorer, too, of gait, of courage lack ;
    Silence a time unbroke.

They walked apart; he of the sturdy gait,
    Was just a little proud,
Reflecting that this stranger was no mate ;
    One of the common crowd.

A garment, too, the richer than the tramp,
    (He better every way);
For see how it keeps out the wind and damp
    From his superior clay.

But what is this, the inner lining cold
    Like ice against his breast ?
Why, one would think its every separate fold
    Gripped like an iron vest.

The chill was piercing to his very heart,
    A mystery he would solve ;
He took it off, and felt its every part,
    A tiny rent evolved

Just near the outer hem, in half exact.
    A flash! inspired! Divine!
The man of courage now no bravery lacked.
    In two the cloak to line

Was rent; then, with rough courtesy, he took,
    Handed his brother poor,
Saying, like shy man, with averted look,
    "Twill help thee 'cross this moor."

A startled look of mingled agony   .
    Swept over that dun face;
And in his throat a rusted "Thanks to ye,"
    Unwilling, lack'd of grace.

E'en this, the other quickly waving back,
    Signed they should nearer walk;
His every impulse now, on better tack;
    Made for some kind of talk.

Besides, the remnant of the cloak began
    To cast about him heat,
A glow so fine, within a little span;
    On wings his words, his feet.

Began to wile away the road with song,
    Then saw, with sudden glance,
A look of anguish lingering there so long,
    He seemed in terror's trance.

Drew near to his companion, seized his hand,
    "Tell me the thing you fear?"
"Oh, God! oh, God! You've manned me and unmann'd;
    Listen, and you shall hear.

"Through poverty and sickness I have kept
    My good name all intact;
But driven hard, I near a gulf had stept,
    My sin has not been fact.

" And when you freely gave, and kindly spoke,
    A sudden light revealed ;
Conscience was roused, as by a mighty stroke,
    Before my fall was sealed.

" And while my life does last, this piece of stuff
    Shall never part from me ;
If I can find no honest work enough,
    Starvation, death, let be."

To comfort him (he shook with such distress),
    The other cried, " Hush, hush,
'Twas not so bad as that, 'twill soon be less,
    Yield not, nor spirit crush."

No fur-lined cloak had he, the comforted,
    But by a lovely law
 A greater glow than any garment shed ;
    Body and soul did thaw.

The poor man then the poorer took in hand,
    And gave himself no rest
Till on his journey to another land ;
    Earnest to do his best.

Long years went by, and on a field of gold
    Luck brought a goodly store.
He'd ever and anon the cloak unfold,
    Recall the past once more.

No sermon had the giver ever preached,   ·
    But *it* had never stayed,
And to the hearer's heart it always reached ;
    Just this rough fragment frayed.

Fear overcame him sometimes as he gazed,
    But oftener 'twas love,
And grateful happy tears, as he, amazed,
    The rescue it did prove.

One day he made resolve to turn him back
    To where that friend still dwelt,
And see if he of this world's goods had lack ;
    Great longing in him felt.

Slowly the ship was nearing to be wharfed ;
    A paper came aboard,
And the first words in it his vision dwarfed,
    A spirit fine had soared.

Straightway he landed, found the house, where lay
    The husk of noble man,
And asked if he might reverently stay
    Beside it, while to plan.

And round about the form so well-beloved,
    Of cloak a remnant part,
His fancy at the last, the sick man moved,
    To fold it near his heart.

The many flocking for a last kind look
    Knew not the reason why ;
The stranger only just a moment shook ;
    A smile drove out a sigh.

No noisy grief, but many, loving, come
    With gifts, a simple flower
Or none, a look, a tear unbidden some,
    The happy dead man's dower.

The traveller said, " 'Tis not a few are here ;
    Was he a man of mark ?"
" Most worthy to be known, bright actions clear ;
    His deeds shine through the dark.

" The half of all he ever came possessed
  He gave for others' good,
No actual alms-gifts, but the poor distressed,
  Upon their feet he stood.

" And many drawn, by his example fine,
  To do the same good deeds,
The beggar and the alms-giver decline ;
  Men look on them as weeds.

" Man to reclaim ! man to restore ! his cry,
  Our money let's not hold.
Men who are idle let all others fly ;
  Doctrine he taught most bold."

" How shall I fit memorial upraise ? "
  Mused he. " Possessed of gold,
How shall all others I induce to praise ?
  The key I think I hold."

A last long look, and then he went his way
  Far 'cross the mighty deep ;
Sought out the greatest painter of the day,
  Whose work might never sleep.

Told him the story of the parted cloak,
  Told of the bitter rain ;
Told of the deeds that happened at a stroke,
  Begged they might live again.

The artist loved the story, thought it out,
  Pourtrayed it with his hand ;
And multitudes all gathering round about,
  In time it was a strand,

Which wove itself into the hearts of men.
  Some scornful glances cast,
But these were few, the many turned again,
  " 'Tis well these colouis last."

A child his mother asked, " What does it show ?"
  She said, " My child, I ween
That man who loves his brother man shall glow,
  His happiness none glean."

And so my " Story of a Cloak " is brought unto an end,
Methinks the loom on which 'twas wove, an angel bright did
  tend.

Cherry Blossoms.

Spring has well come, and I see
Blossom on the cherry tree ;
Hark ! around it everywhere
Bees are humming in the air.

Pleasant velvet-coated bee,
At thy work so earnestly ;
We must pause a moment, think,
What is the mysterious link ?

Ask the tree what draws the bee
Thwart the sunshine, true as free ?
Man can conquer many things ;
But " to know " hath unclipt wings.

Then the bees are winged away,
Sweetest blossomings decay ;
But the clustering fruit is there ;
How ? Who, answering, can declare ?

Sound the cherry falls asleep
'Neath the curtaining leaves so deep ;
Air and Sun, the nursing pair,
Tend them with unerring care.

Soon the cherry reddening, wakes,
Every day bright colour takes ;
All excitement, men and bird,
Thoughts of feasts are in them stirred.

Deep the mystery of the tree !
Deep the mystery of the bee !
But a deeper mystery still,
Mortals mystery cannot thrill.

Winnie.

No longer glancing comes my way
The Winnie of a former day ;
But while I live I'll not forget ;
The sunny memory lingers yet.

She came to me for mulberry leaves,
Talk'd of the time, the silkworm weaves ;
Soon, gaily wound, the pretty thread,
Fair hand of Youth, was on her head.

But care for silkworms soon must cool,
And fate takes up another spool ;
Now round the heart of Winnie twine
The golden coils of love divine.

Heartsease.

TO B.B.'s PICTURE.

Dost thou, indeed, ease hearts of those who grieve?
And does thy depth of purple softness entering in,
Melt men to sorrow for o'erwhelming sin?
And does thy dew-dimmed eye, so faithful, looking up,
Beguile, like glance from them, while drinking sorrow's cup?
We love thee, and we love to so believe.

And does thy beauteous sister, golden-hued,
Does she tell men of crown they may attain,
When cleansed at last from every earthly stain?
And cheer their hearts, 'neath stress of battle sore,
Till they have ease of heart for evermore?
Then spirit reigns supreme, the flesh subdued.

Answer to "A Vain Cry."*

No longer pine so bitterly and weep
For hours departed; youth's wild passion thrill;
Seek not to bring back forms, now peaceful, still;
Look up! the same blue sky o'er arches deep.
Out from the ashes of that dying fire,
Strive not to call again, pale ghosts of days,
Or 'tis of course, a mournful song they raise;
But watch! and joy will spring from out the pyre.

---

*Mr. C. J. O'Regan's "A Vain Cry," given below, appeared in the Christchu ch
Star. The above answer by L. B. appeared the following week.

And love shall dawn afresh, abiding, grand,
And the dim past, no longer dead, will show
In tapestries of time, all woven ; glow
The burnished gold, and the dark shadows planned.
In one whole, then, will all thy life be bound
By thought; which is not either young or old ;
Graves all are empty, save of worm and mould,
Shroud not Spirit, and Life ? like circle, round.

A Vain Cry.

By C. J. O'Regan.

I sometimes turn from these grey days that be
Backward unto the fair days once I knew,
The far, fair days when all the world seemed true,
Ere yet I learned that Joy had wings to flee.
" Oh Days !" I cry, " so wonderful and blue,
Come back again, come back and bring to me
The silent laughter and the vanished glee.
Come back, dear Days, I swear to cherish you ! "

Then back on me with sad, reproachful eye,
Each old Day looks and voices without sound
Come from them : " Mortal, cease that bootless cry ;
We came to you bliss-laden and we crowned
Your soul with joys, and after all we found,
You blest us not, but smiled to see us die."

Golden Poetry.

In many a one there's lies a vein
      Of golden Poetry ;
He knows it not; no outward stain
      Reveals the mystery.

He says, " Maybe, I have no spade
      To dig so deeply down ; "
No youthful hopes ? no joys that fade ?
No crown of Love hast known."

A lovely sight, a glorious sound,
      Divining rod did make ;
Then guessed ye not, beneath the ground,
      The gold that made it shake ? "

"No ! " for ye said, " 'Tis not my bent,
      This treasure-trove to seek ;
In gaining living, Life is spent,
      Poetic store, a freak ! "

Sometimes a lovely soul, gold-strown,
      Will easily reveal ;
The poetry of life is shown,
      And needs no minting seal.

The digger knows his brother-kind,
      And soon a comrade spies;
For gold, they crush the earthy rind,
      Wash glittering sand that lies.

Joy Hath a Shadow.

Joy hath a shadow falling very dark,
For oftentimes our joy's high water-mark
Is lessened very sore, because we know
A friend's kind face withdraws an answering glow.

In sorrow, friends will better mourn with thee,
And dole thy wreck, and make thee sadder be ;
But when thou look'st, that thy joy bright their eye,
They turn away, not bearing see thee high.

Oh ! when thou happy, find'st a tender friend
Who, seeing thee all glad, more glad will tend,
Be sure that thou hast found no common one ;
A great heart beats, and thou art not alone.

None need another grudge his sight of Joy,
That brilliant guest, fleet-footed, wing'd, and coy ;
So rapid passes 'cross our disc of days,
Then, turned to grub, for long most quiet stays.

Why, why do we, in this short span of time,
Not suffer sympathy to set the chime ?
And so rejoice with him who laugheth gay,
That we ourselves, from dulness, snatch a day.

To-day.

To-day ! we hold it in our hands,
    As child folds fast
    Some wee wild bird ;
When hands in sleep we careless fling,
Devouring night on day will spring.

How vast the pile of days that went
    To make a base
    For this to-day !
An apex for a few short hours,
Then o'er it just one other towers.

To-day ! the flower of all the days,
    Some lightly prize
    And scatter free ;
Seeds of past days are garnered home,
And cherished ; buds of days to come.

To-day ! keystone of lofty arch
    That springs beneath
    The hand of Time,
And joins the Past, we partly know,
To Future, mist-enveloped bow.

'Twas said by mighty Emperor,
    " That if ' To-day '
    Went by unstarred
By deed of mercy, it was lost !"
A nobler saying lips ne'er crossed.

Sometimes a mortal, fairy-touched,
    Makes golden threads
    Of bright to-day,
And weaves them in a garment fair ;
Such texture is the moth's despair.

A Dream.

OF LIFE, OF DEATH, AND AFTER.

    Majestic king of wave,
    Cresting towards the shore,
    As though the earth a slave
    He loved to lord it o'er ;
A beckoning finger seemed to me
To make my home upon the sea.

I built my hut quite near,
And each day loved to sight
The ships that passed, and hear
Voices, and look for light;
But, oh! I longed that I might be
A happy sailor on the sea.

On land I had my work
So I might bread to eat;
The wolf I'd known to lurk,
And hard he is to cheat;
But when I loosened from the strain
Towards the sea again, again.

I swam a little way
From off the sandy shore
One glorious summer day,
Sea said, " Return no more."
And I? As blithe as blithe could be,
Just floundering in the lovely sea.

Some fear came o'er me when
No craft came, took me in,
For, like all other men,
Some boat-room I must win,
When gladly, joyfully I spied
A spar of wood near, on the tide.

It bore me up by day,
And in the night the stars
Looked kindly on my way,
The least of ocean's tars;
Though oft the sea engulfed me o'er,
I never turned my face to shore.

Sometimes men looked and laughed
From the great solemn ships,
At how I made a raft
With planks, and ends, and chips ;
But when I stood on it and steered,
And raised my sail, I no more feared.

For the same breeze that fills
The sails of all the ships,
Steals down the high wave hills
And speeds the raft of chips ;
Enough it was for me, I knew
That salt-sea winds around me blew.

And beauteous sights I saw,
And many lessons learned ;
One, kindness is a law
Sometimes on great ships spurned.
And only wreck, and loss, and pain
Teach some men how to sail the main.

Oft from a leaky boat
One pulls a spar to throw
A man but just afloat,
O'er lightless turns a glow ;
And many a one has jumped to save
His sinking brother from the wave.

I never owned a boat,
But all my life content,
Just kept my raft afloat,
And when my strength was spent,
I laid me down and fell asleep ;
So death, one night, the watch did keep.

But I awoke again,
Again was in the sea ;
This—this was not the main
I knew ; it could not be !
Grand, more beautiful, peaceful too,
And as my eyes grew strong, light grew.

Then He who rules the main,
Crafts, and the hands aboard,
Saw me, all weather-stain,
And quick a boat was lowered ;
I felt ashamed to come so poor,
But just a kind face looked me o'er.

I murmured some few words,
" I never gained a place,
Some planks, bound with some cords,
And out of every race,
The great ships passed me day by day,
I low amongst the waves, alway."

" Did'st thou ne'er place thy sail
To catch the heavenly wind ?
Nor face the tempter pale ?
Nor do good deed, or kind ?"
" I did my raft try steer aright,
And loved some few, and made some fight."

" Then thou shalt have a barque ;
Try thou to steer it well ;
Thy captain speakest, hark !
The thankful chorus swell."
" And can it be that I shall sail
This goodly ship, and no more fail ?"

Marguerite in Golden Hair.

To a Picture.

Can painter picture forth a dream more fair,
    Sweet Marguerite,
Than thou, entwined in glinting golden hair,
    That sunbeams greet?
When sight so perfect meets our seeing eyes,
They, resting, know a satisfied surprise.

The silver of the flower-cup is so dead;
    From it we glance
To the warm whiteness of the clear forehead;
    Blue veins enhance,
Marking that purity alone is cold,
Till Love, her sister, round her, arms enfold.

Beyond the guarded fortress of thy life,
    Dost thou look out,
And think of her, who perished in the strife,
    Goëthe wrote about?
She gave the lovely flower its lovely name,
And him, no slender part, of his great fame.

She gently pulled to pieces, scattering round,
    Immortal bloom!
'Twas born on wind and fell upon the ground;
    E'en so her doom;
She, lost amidst the fierceness of the storm,
Aroused by evil one in mocking form.

Now, when we look on it, we think of her,
    And tears well up;
Slow falling on the flower, its beauty blurr,
    And fill the cup
As her's was filled, so full of grief and wrong,
That o'er her story, we muse, pondering, long.

The Morn Cloud.

The smiling sun had gathered morning mist,
In vapoury clouds that rolled on many a hill,
And then away, save one that did insist,
Below the summit of a peak, and fill
Each slender grass-blade, fuller than the rest, with clear rain-
        dew.

The hills rejoiced that shone the soonest 'neath
The radiance of that shimmering day,
And pitied one, low cloud so long did wreath
And hold enwrapped in watery, tearful sway ;
The voice of whispering winds came near, and back their
•   judgment blew.

Then, when the setting sun bathed bright their sides,
'Twas noted that the grass grew greener there,
And beautiful the slope the morn-cloud hides,
O'er brooding, close and long, with tenderest care :
So, glad the hill, that shadow left, enriched a deeper hue.

And tender mothers sought this grassy spot,
And led their pretty lambs to feed and sleep,
And, in their way, gave thanks for pleasant lot
To Him who shepherds winds, and hills, and sheep ;
So all of these sang soft and low as on calm evening drew.

Henrietta.

At close of day, I passed a place
Where " evening-primrose " one did rear ;
Forthwith, uprose a dear friend's face,
By memory pencill'd, swift and clear.

She, pale and graceful as the flower,
Drooped, and was gathered from our eyes;
Death looped the curtain, lost his power,
She greeting found in Paradise.

There waits to welcome those she loves,
Her only grief they grieve so sore,
The faithful " It is well " but proves
That Love is Love for evermore.

Suggested by Synod, 1894.

Because no longer names of saints we 'rol
On lettered days, or 'grave on parchment scroll,
Do they cease live, for ever mingling in,
And bright exempling forth, turn men from sin ?

. Does the salt ocean leave off purifying,
Or washing tides pause ever their replying,
Because that we its drops can never count,
Or gauge the heighth and depth of waves that mount ?

Does the great sun cease shining on his course
Because no mortal man can trace his source,
Or ever hope, to numbering, count his rays ?
We rest content, glad that he gives us days.

Does Spring retard, or cease to re-appear
E'en if we note not buds, or unsheath'd spear ?
Or Summer, if we mark not Rose's leaf,
And limn the flowers, so beautiful and brief ?

Does Autumn ripen not her countless seeds,
If some of her great harvest measure needs?
Or winter keep him back his wholesome frost
Because, ere we can trace it, it is lost?

So it remains for man to perfect learn
That goodness *is*, and even though some spurn,
Remains essential, leavens, fructifies
In human hearts, and, ever battling cries.

The Milky Way.

Emboss'd against their marvellous shield, the tender blue of
    night,
I saw the bright stars gleaming forth, bedewing earth with
    light ;
And as I watched them long, and mused, glad thoughts my
    mind possessed,
That these are like good deeds of men, that stand by men
    confessed.
By Fame such deeds have been enwrought on her vast banner's
    furl,
And moulded by the poet's thought, in songs, whose words are
    pearl.
But soon a cloud of sadness dimmed this joyous mood of mine,
For I guessed at deeds of mercy, on which no light may shine,
Lost in the stormy chaos whirl of poverty and sin,
And drowned, with wrecked lives, amidst the tempest and its
    din.

Who records of the hungry, that he gave his piece of bread ?
Or tells of shivering mortals, who their garment wider spread ?
Of sorrowful, who smiling went, and cheered full many an one ?
Of tired-out worker who did more, for fainting friend to atone ?
Of traveller in the desert, who gave water, precious drops ?
Of wounded soldier, whose weak arm, a dying comrade props ?
Of mother of the many mouths, who yet has nobly striven
To fold the lonely orphan child, for whom her heart is riven ?
Of captive bending 'neath his load, yet helps companion weak ?
Oh ! multitudes of deeds there are, of which we never speak.
Such deeds by men of every race, of every tongue and clime,
We know are done, and will be done, till end is made of time.

A gentle rustling at my side, a voice so soft and kind,
A finger pointing to the sky, and words float on the wind :
" Besides the stars, dost thou not see, across the arching blue,
A pathway streaming pure and white ?   It answer gives to
     you ;
'Tis symbol shadowing forth His way, who made men brave for
     right;
And sets their deeds, in Heaven of Heavens, for ever in His
     sight.
The unknown deeds of faith and love, the weak sad ones have
     done,
In streams of Light that grow more light, He gathers round
     His throne.
God knows all hearts, and every deed, exactly what it cost,
The brightest glittering as a star, no hidden one is lost."

I, now alone, watch many a star, that grandly gives its ray,
Then turn, with exquisite delight, to trace the Milky Way.

To Evelyn.

Maiden at maturity!
Thou are launched upon Life's sea;
And I pray thy little boat
On a sunny sea may float.

May the winds be always fair,
And the waves that do thee bear,
Ever roll towards the shore,
Where is parting never more.

May Love, seated in the barque,
Cheer thee when the days are dark;
May thy heart's desire be filled,
If by Heaven it is so willed.

Look for Love in many a guise,
And for it all else despise;
Gold is good, and fame is grand;
Minus Love, thy boat may strand.

If thou art thy mother's child,
Thou wilt never far be guiled
From the path of duty bright;
She has passed thee on a light.

But should roughening winds and waves
Toss thee near to rocky caves,
Be not overcome of things;
E'en adversity has wings.

And when thou the shore hast reached,
And thy boat is safely beached,
May the friends that thou wouldst see,
Everyone be greeting thee!

Wishing.

Why should mankind for ever wish
Their friends a dainty mental dish ?
Nay ! rather wish them opening eyes,
Until the day of death's surprise.

Yes ! when the heart's desire is stilled,
Most surely then a grave is filled ;
On wings of wishing, men should rise,
Till from the earth, cease anguished cries.

Content ! we take thee by the throat
Till every man is in the boat ;
And on the sea of life is seen,
No more the shipwrecked " might-have-been."

" Thy Brother's Blood."

The wrongs that men have done to men are like the seeding
weed,
Which, trampled in the ground, or scattered on the wind, none
heed.

Wrongdoers close their eyes and say, " These will not rise
again."
We know the words are like the men who say them, vain, in
vain.

A countless host, how mightily they spring from out the
ground,
Each one an arméd band that chokes the fruitful soil around.

Sadly the reapers come, perforce, and the rank bundles bind,
Lo ! 'midst them bitter blood, salt tears, and poison flowers
they find.

"They that Sow in Tears."

In sorrow man goes forth again, this time good grain to sow,
His tears are mingled with the seed that feeds the furrow low.

He waits with patience, 'though the tempters say, " See all is
    gone,
Unfruitful seed on barren ground, it will abide alone."

But in due time forth from the earth shall glorious harvests
    spring,
The teeming plains shall laugh aloud, and all the valleys sing.
Glad reapers, bearing golden sheaves, shall stand before the
    King.

A Christmas Idyl.

Pity bent low before the King of Kings;
She said, " Lord, it is near the Christmas-tide
When earth rejoices, for alway it brings
A flood of thought so bright, our griefs we hide.

" I come to plead that Thou wilt yet once more
Ope hearts and unclose hands, that all may feast,
For this there's need that wealth unlock its store,
So, men, be satisfied, e'en to the very least."

Then the great King gave Pity answer, saying,
" Before thy words were spoken, wish expressed,
Thou wast heard; go, anxious fears, allaying;
Hearts are made ready for thyself, the guest."

So Pity went in haste, with utmost speed,
Her soft brown eyes, wide-open, glistened ;
So bright, as full of ungathered tears indeed,
She saw, heard enough for weeping, so she looked and listened.

Did well her work, made rich men give, so bountifully, free,
The poorest on Christ's day did live, and feast right royally.

But Justice, standing up before the King,
Said, " I would ask of thee, oh ! mighty Lord,
That not at Christmas time alone, men sing,
But all men at all times, with one accord,

" Eat and have food enough, each day that comes,
All have a share of dainties earth doth grow ;
Work each man every day, go forth from happy homes,
So Heaven be not far off, but here below.

" I would that not the few be surfeited,
And live at ease, exempt from wholesome toil ;
Or that the rest, see never work completed,
Nor know of leisure ; fight, but share not spoil."

" Justice, because that thou hast bandaged eyes,
And cannot see how all things, working, tend
Towards the balancing of things all wise,
So in the meantime, Pity, needs must mend.

" Long centuries ago, a bright light shined,
And ever since, men's eyes are growing to see ;
But whirling dust of motives, spinning, blind,
And only Time evolves man just and free.

"Still o'er the chaos, bright the glorious sun has risen ;
His rays increase, clouds may arise, but light cannot
        imprison."

Little Sketches.

EASTER DAY—WINCHESTER CATHEDRAL.

In sacred building, long ago,
I heard a choir-boy sing " I know."
I cannot hope to hear that strain
So gloriously sung again ;
It rang adown the archéd nave,
And reached the roof, as tidal wave ;
One felt Death's shadow fade away,
And saw the Resurrection ray!

WRITING.

Think thine own thoughts,
See with thine own eyes,
Have human feeling in the heart ;
And words,
Words will come, a glad and sweet surprise.

SUNSHINE ON THE SNOW.

I see the sun shine on the snow,
And lo !
A wilderness of diamonds glow,
Quick images, my mind o'erflow,
But no !
I wean myself from all,
And not a glance bestow ;
E'en so.

The snow, it is pure white,
The gems made by the light;
Men may long words indite;
The simplest I will write,
A child in it's delight,
" Oh ! what a pretty sight."

VANITY.

Intently, Vanity looks half her time within,
    And thinks of admiration she would win;
The other half, she casts her lines around,
    And tries to fill a bag, that has no bound.

LONELINESS.

A poor old woman lived alone; she died,
And at her death no kindly mortal cried;
So from on high an angel softly came,
And shed bright tears for one none cared to name.

TEARS.

The tears of men that fall,
Arise in misty cloud;
Their fair blue sky enthral,
Their joyous hopes enshroud.
These clouds above them break,
Descend in pleasant showers;
We'll love them for the sake
Of all the loveliest flowers.

CHRISTCHURCH—MAY MORNING.

Pink upon the velvet hills,
Pink upon the rising spire,
Pink upon the lark that trills,
But only one, the pink t' admire.

AN EFFECT—NEW BRIGHTON.

O'er the horizon spreads a blue-black cloud ;
Sun's slanting rays light up the nearer shore ;
The gathered waters break, as the beach is ploughed,
In glittering streams, like molten silver ore.

FANNY.

Fanny of the chestnut hair,
Colour that the painters dare ;
Mist of curls about thy head,
Might be, by the west wind, spread.

Out from 'neath the hair, thine eyes,
Look at one with such surprise !
Well they may, for Life is new ;
On thee rests the morning dew.

DAY'S DRESS.

Robe that the storm-cloud flingeth wide,
Day's dress of beauty long may hide ;
But we know she weareth blue,
From every rift it peepeth through.

Peter Bell.

EPISODE IN A KINDERGARTEN.

I have a tale to tell,
It is of Peter Bell;
His teacher with a searching glance,
As up and down she'd proudly prance,
Said, " Peter Bell, keep time, 1, 2, 3."

He tried to do it well,
Poor little Peter Bell;
E'en then would stream her flowing mane,
She'd still repeat, in accents plain,
" Peter Bell, keep time, 1, 2, 3."

This same young Peter Bell
Was every inch a " swell ; "
For this she did'nt care a bit ;
If he showed " side," she'd on him " sit,"
With " Peter Bell, keep time, 1, 2, 3."

Sometimes our Peter Bell
Would very loudly yell,
At sight of a great big thick stick,
And at a voice that said so quick,
" Peter Bell, keep time, 1, 2, 3."

He said, " I will rebel,"
This dauntless Peter Bell,
In frying-pan of loftiest scorn,
She fried poor Bell, that self-same morn ;
And " Peter Bell, keep time, 1, 2, 3."

" This teacher I will fell,"
Planned brave boy, Peter Bell ;
But when he up, and would so durst,
She seemed as though for blood to thirst,
And " Peter Bell, keep time, 1, 2, 3."

So vanquished, Peter Bell,
Said, " Life is just a sell,"
His teacher said, " you idle child,
To-day I'll only put it mild,
Peter Bell, keep time, 1, 2, 3."

At last, for Peter Bell
They rang a doleful knell ;
In agonies of grief she came,
And breathing forth his pretty name,
In faltering voice she could not tame,
" He always did his part so well,
Did curly-headed Peter Bell,
And ever marched his 1, 2, 3,
With step elastic, proud and free."

The ghost of Peter Bell
Went up on high to dwell ;
He caught his sorrowing teacher's words,
It cheered him, though his blood was curds ;
He kept time flying, 1, 2, 3.

He rang his namesake's bell,
Did shadowy Peter Bell ;
St. Peter met him, very square,
" Why, what a mite, to knock and dare,
And how about this 1, 2, 3 ? "

Then up spake Peter Bell,
" I always stept it well."
St. Peter bent his noble knee
To pat this child so full of glee,
And said, " It's very clear to me,
Your teacher never went on spree ;
To you my welcome is most free,
But don't forget your 1, 2, 3."

So jolly little Peter Bell
  Has finished quite his earthly spell ;
His teacher now, in accents mild,
Oft says to every other child,   ´
    " I wish you'd seen my Peter Bell,
    He did his 1, 2, 3 so well."

——————

The Breakfast Room.

(Founded on fact.)

Some love the glorious mountain-top,
Some rave about the valley's drop ;
Some dwell upon the sunlit plain ;
Some long for sight of sea again ;
A pictured dream will ever loom
For some, a little breakfast-room.

'Tis small, and all around it books.
This party in them seldom looks ;
As in and out the graces glide,
The writer's apt to let work slide ;
Besides, they breakfast on and off,
And 'tween times, take a snack of toff.

In that same room, a writer sits ;
He thinks in starts, and writes in fits ;
He slashes " Times," impacts the " Star,"
But other times, his thoughts are far ;
He loves to breakfast and to dream
Where beauty reigns, and reigns supreme.

The Graces hover round him then,
And say "A moment leave the pen;"
They draw for him a nice arm-chair,
Say, "Rest your burning brow, lean there,
"And we will bring a bit of toast,
"At breakfast—you'll not care for roast."

There's sprightly Connie, who will dare
To laugh when asked her heart to spare;
And Annie, with the sun-bright glance,
That pencilled brows above, enhance;
And Hebe, tall and dignified,
She walketh in her maiden pride.

There's A. A. Donis, plain and neat
From crown of head to sole of feet;
We look upon his face again,
But there, we must not make men vain
Besides, they're going to breakfast now;
Girls will giggle, chance a row.

Sometimes the room is filled with cloud,
A veteran smoker might be proud;
One ladles his tobacco out,
In turns they fill the pipe, or pout;
Then all is scattered in great haste,
For breakfast comes, no time to waste.

Sometimes they draw around the fire,
And after poetry enquire;
The gentle youth then reads quite soft,
And silence reigns two minutes, oft;
Then hunger seizes them again;
"We want some breakfast," they explain.

The little wingéd god is near,
And looks for some poor heart to spear;
His bow is bent, his arrow fixed,
He aims to hit the armour 'twixt;
But in the sheaf, it goes once more;
These breakfasts are to him a bore.

For dinner, there's no appetite;
The common room puts all to flight;
They try to talk on general things,
And wish the dinner went on wings;
'Tis done! they joyful wend their way,
And for dessert, bring breakfast-tray.

This scene is drawing to a close;
On earth we never know repose,
For breakfast-rooms must pass away;
Stern dining, it has come to stay;
Romance was in those meals they shared,
For breakfasting, was all they cared.

All About a Brush.

A MODERATELY TRUE STORY.

It was so like a thrush,
  That beautiful new brush;
It went with such a rush,
  When it only had a push.

The Wind was much impressed!
"A bird is on its nest!"
  So just in playful jest,
He blew, we know the rest.

But when he saw it did'nt fly,
    He said, it sounded like " My eye!
There'll be a row to reach the sky;
    I think I'll bid this scene good-bye."

A pup, he jumped for joy,
    He saw that brush so coy;
" A bone I will deploy,
    Just some one to annoy;

    " My mother buries bones;
    Now for a heap of stones;
There will be many groans,
    But fun for all atones."

Miss Oakwon had a plan;
    Hired a scientific man;
He had not long began,
    When against the brush he ran.

" Oh! isn't this a store?
    Why, brushes were of yore!
No doubt the Maoris had some more:
    I'll hide it, or 'twill end in gore."

To the museum softly crept,
    " See! 'tis a treasure I have kept,"
Into his mouth, his heart then leapt,
    For archæologic joy he wept!

This isn't new, there are a score
    Of tales 'bout brushes, ancient lore;
If you find time but to explore,
    You'll come upon them! yes! galore.

How Nice 'twould be.

How nice 'twould be if Mrs. A. were not a gad-about,
Or better still, if Mrs. B. would leave her phrases out ;
A grand, good thing if Mrs. C. would do her household work,
A blessed change if Mrs. D. made phrases like to Burke,
A providence if Mrs. E. would mind her children more,
And economical Miss F. kept groceries in store.
If wretched risen Mrs. G. were not so ignorant,
And that good soul, dear Mrs. H. were perfect free from cant.
How pleasant if friend Mrs. I. were not so full of I,
And, too, if Mrs. J. did not on all her neighbours spy.
A real advance if Mrs. K. did not so proudly soar,
More suitable, if Mrs. L. did not herself so lower.
And if that pretty Mrs. M. would leave off dancing quite,
Sweet Mrs. N. would have a chance of softening her spite.
We wish, indeed, that Mrs. O. would waive her crockery's cost,
That Mrs. P., her ancestors, in the Red Sea had lost.
If Mrs. Q. had in her youth but married all her beaux,
Then Mrs. R. need not show tired, because their number grows.
Could Mrs. S. pursuaded be to dress herself with taste,
And Mrs. T. not always screw her tiny little waist.
If Mrs. U. would fill her mind with something else than fads,
More dignified if Mrs. V. left fussing silly lads.
Why does not Mrs. W. for weaknesses allow ?
And Mrs. X. be quieter ; it's nicer, not a row !
Oh ! Mrs. Y. do tell us less, about your servant woes,
And last, not least, dear Mrs. Z., just keep off other's toes.

Then what a perfect world we'd have,
If all were put in mould,
And no one ever made mistake,
So nothing left to scold ;
Like fish on land, we'd gasp about,
And long for turbid water, like the trout.

www.ingramcontent.com/pod-product-compliance
Lightning Source LLC
Chambersburg PA
CBHW021245260626
47172CB00002B/850